I0672429

Whispers Across the Sea

Love never lets go

P. A. Farrell

ISBN:

The Pocket Companion Series contains:

When Your Mind Won't Stop

After the Loss: Finding Your Way Through Grief

You Are Enough: Rebuilding Your Self-Worth

At the Crossroads: Making Decisions When Nothing Feels Clear

When People Hurt: Navigating Difficult Relationships

When You Feel Stuck: Finding Movement in Hard Times

Books by Patricia A. Farrell, Ph.D.

When You Can't Pour From an Empty Glass: CBT Skills for Exhausted Caregivers

The Little Book on Learning Big Critical Thinking Skills

The Smart Kid's Survival Guide: Making Good Choices in a Confusing World

How to Be Your Own Therapist

P. A. FARRELL

It's Not All in Your Head: Anxiety, Depression, Mood Swings and Multiple Sclerosis

Unfiltered: Beneath the noise of our thoughts lies the true narrative of our minds

Unfiltered Again: A behind-the-scenes look at healthcare, medicine and mental health

A Social Security Disability Psychological Claims Handbook: A simple guide to understanding your SSD claim for psychological impairments and unraveling the maze of decision-making

A Social Security Disability Psychological Claims Guidebook for Children's Benefits

The Disability Accessible US Parks in All 50 States: A Comprehensive Guide

Birding in the US NOW!: A birding guide for individuals with disabilities

Contents

Chapter 1: The Voice Beneath the Waves

Driving along the lonely road, she tried to keep her mind empty of anything and just allow what she was seeing in front of her to be all and nothing more. Up ahead, the road narrowed to crunching gravel as it reached the headland, with small shining bits of stone shouting out in the afternoon sun. To her right, the ocean extended as a metallic surface that caught sunlight before its waves exploded into their own depths. The air made a constant breathing sound that seemed to exist before human memory started. So surreal and yet so predictable in its consistent rhythm. Was this to be home? If so, for how long?

Irene reduced her speed as she approached the white cottage atop the hill. Sure enough, the house was still there, but in a weathered condition, with its uneven shutters and exposed wooden surface, that the ocean wind had left exposed to the elements. Still, the house maintained a strong presence, as if it had been waiting for her arrival.

A smile crossed her face as she considered that the house had been waiting for her. Waiting indeed.

She pulled up next to the weathered and worn mailbox that marked the cottage with its faded letters. Once, of course, they had been fresh and lively, but now they showed years of battering by wind and rain. But the number was still enough to be read by any passer-by seeking this cottage. It had not lost its place to the weather.

The atmosphere greeted her with a combination of ocean salt and freezing temperatures. Irene took a deep breath of the salty air, believing it would cleanse her inner self. She had spent seven hours driving from the city to reach this place. At the same time, she left behind her previous self, who believed in permanent relationships, including marriage and family, and the belief that grief would end. Here, she was hoping that if grief didn't end, at least it would soften. Grief, after all, had thrown itself over her as a leaden blanket of emotion. She wasn't sure she could get herself out from under it.

Her sister's death had showed her that grief doesn't have an endpoint. The hospital environment had produced a persistent background noise while her sister's last spoken words and her fading breath created an unidentifiable void that followed her throughout her days. The breakdown of her marriage developed at a slow pace until she lost the ability to fight against its progression. So much had happened, and she needed something, but she didn't know what. Perhaps it was here. At least, she hoped it might be here.

She stood at the ocean's edge while the stiff breeze pulled at her clothing and hair as she sought complete peace. Peace was what she was seeking but at this moment, the ocean was reluctant.

The stairs on the cottage's front porch creaked and almost groaned as she ascended them as though they resented the effort. Opening the door was a pleasant return to the familiar household aromas, which combined the aging of timber with lavender and a hint of smoke. The scents of her aunt were in the air, indicating she was close by. Quickly, Irene put that thought out of her mind. Her aunt couldn't be present and hadn't been here for some time now.

But the atmosphere inside the house seemed to belong to the people who had lived there. It seemed to be waiting for her return when the ocean tide would arrive. The scene brought back all her previous visits to this place where she used to sit and talk and walk along the beach. Yes. Calm. Comforting.

She stayed motionless for several seconds after entering the house. Its silence had a textured quality, like a handmade blanket that spanned the space. The mantel clock kept sounding a steady tick while the wooden beams made faint noises, and the ocean waves pressed their sounds against the building seawalls. She dropped her suitcase to the floor after taking a deep breath.

Her aun't cottage had maintained its original appearance since her childhood visits, with its uneven shelves holding seashells, the worn quilt covering the armchair, and the oversized watercolor painting of the sea. A small laugh signaled that she agreed her aunt had chosen an oversized frame for the seascape, but that didn't matter. The room had a new sound that wasn't produced by machines, nor did it resemble any known noise—a kind of awareness. It was almost as though the house were watching her, and she didn't know how she felt about that. Maybe it was just fatigue from the long drive or what she had been through recently that was priming these ideas in her head.

Enough with the initial focus on the room's details, she thought. Now, she turned her attention to the shortwave radio resting on a small table in the corner. It was another familiar piece of the room's furnishings. The radio showed its age through its unpolished dials and a slightly warped antenna, but this didn't affect its operation. It had belonged to her aunt.

Irene smiled faintly. Her aunt used to spend her evenings searching for unusual radio signals, claiming to receive messages from distant locations, ships, and foreign lands. The existence of supernatural entities that could be reached through radio waves remained unclear to her. Irene didn't know, but the idea kept coming back to her as she looked at the radio. There was no reason to be scared, and she felt interested instead.

Ghosts. A brief image of that flashed through her mind before she chose to ignore it.

The word stayed in her mind despite her attempts to push it away. She walked to the other side of the room while running her fingers across the radio's top edge. The metal surface felt cool to the touch with its dust particles and tiny sand grains. She pulled her hand back immediately after feeling the radio produce a faint static vibration through her skin. The electrical charge from memory seemed to create this illusion, but there was no actual signal present. Odd that the radio should suddenly do that. Again, she dismissed any thought of something other than errant electricity.

She laughed at her own jitters while saying to herself, "You're on edge, Irene, because the house doesn't have ghosts, but you're exhausted."

But the room became heavier with an invisible presence when she walked to the window. The presence didn't feel heavy or threatening, but it existed in the space. A presence?

The sky outside turned a mix of lilac and slate as dusk approached. The ocean waves continued their steady movement until they reached the shore, where they transformed into foam that moved up the rocks before retreating slowly. They moved with perfect precision and created a soothing musical sound that brought comfort.

She moved about automatically, placing sweaters into drawers, her book on the nightstand, and her sister's photo near the lamp. The photograph brought an intense feeling of sadness. Her sister was more than missed, and she stopped for a moment to stare. There was no doubt that she would always miss her.

Almost instinctively she spoke to the empty space in a whisper, saying, "You would have loved this place." She recalled her sister's words about the sea and its ability to create stability. Her sister had been with her through all her travels because she was always by her side. She wanted to keep this special bond with her, and she refused to break it.

Just there, the kettle started making a hissing sound after she almost forgot that she'd turned it on for tea. A peaceful sound of the kettle floated in the air as another calming force that brought her back to reality. She held the tea mug with both hands while returning to where the radio was.

Her aunt's memories float into her mind like a rising ocean wave. The old woman spoke with a pleasant smile while saying to Irene, "The air contains memories, which you can hear if you listen for a long time." She needed to listen for an extended period to retrieve some of her lost memories. But would anything else also come to her?

Irene extended her hand toward the radio before stopping to turn one of its dials. Only static that sounded like a soft crackling sound came out of its speaker. She moved the dial again before trying the next one. Then the static changed into a rhythmic pattern that sounded like distant waves or human breathing.

Slowly, she moved her face closer to the radio and spoke in a playful tone, asking, "Is anyone there?" There would be both shock and happiness if someone replied to her question. But no one answered.

The static now sounded a deep exhale before the line went silent. Then there was a pause that made her doubt if she had really heard it before a faint click sound followed by a word that sounded like it came from a voice through mist. Was that a sound? A voice?

Her heart started racing rapidly. She moved closer to the radio. "Hello?" She doubted that anyone would answer her calls, but she wished for a connection, so she spoke into the void.

The radio signal lapsed into complete silence after the static vanished. No one was there.

Irene returned to her seat feeling slightly self-conscious about her racing heart. The signal probably originated from a distant fishing boat or a still-active weather broadcast. Yet she refused to accept this explanation even though she knew it was true. It felt like there must be something else.

She put the radio back on the table before walking to the window. The full moon shone brightly in the sky, creating a wavering path across the ocean surface. The wind ruffled her hair, bringing scents of ocean salt and metallic notes that reminded her of aged coins and corroded metal. In that moment, she thought of the combination of old houses with their surrounding ocean and how they created a special blend of mystery and enchantment.

Then, she detected the same sound again. No, she hadn't been mistaken this time. Maybe before, but not now.

The voice emerged from the air instead of the radio while speaking in a deep, measured tone that seemed patient. "You're not alone."

Somewhat surprised, she remained motionless with the mug held in her hands. The soft spoken words reached her ears but she could have ignored them, something she chose not to do. The words brought a sense of comfort that felt like a gentle touch on her shoulder.

She spoke into the darkness "Who are you?"

The waves outside produced a continuous drumming sound, but no answer emerged from the silence.

Standing motionless for an extended period while her breathing became shallow, she mentally searched for an answer. The sensation of warmth remained on her skin as if the surrounding air retained some form of memory. Thinking about sorting out her clothing, she went to the bedroom where her suitcase was still on the bed.

Returning to the living room after several minutes, she found the radio's red dial softly glowing although she hadn't turned it on or maybe she had touched it by accident. The kettle stopped hissing because she must have turned it off. No one would make tea while keeping the stove flame on.

The room became completely silent after the wind stopped rattling the windows. Laughing weakly, she said, "Enough, Irene, because you need rest and you've lost too much. Your brain creates these sounds because you want to hear them." It was as much reassurance as she could provide to herself, and yet she wanted something more.

Returning to the couch, she noticed the kettle on the stove had stopped steaming, although she already knew she hadn't turned it off. She must have turned it off. Hadn't she? The room became completely silent at that moment. Her heartbeat was the only sound she could hear while a soft and steady hum existed beneath it.

She kept her eyes shut to focus on the sounds, remembering what her aunt had told her. The presence she detected through the radio, ghostly energy, or divine power no longer made her feel afraid. The presence brought her peace.

She remained unsure about the identity of the voice she heard because it could have belonged to a person who used to stand by this window in the past while listening to the wind and speaking into the radio. Perhaps a sailor lost his ship in the nearby ocean waters while his messages disappeared during the intense storm. The man continued to send messages through the air even after his ship sank. No, that was too much of a stretch, and she didn't want to let her mind go there.

Irene finished her tea before placing the mug down and spoke into the dark space, "Goodnight to whoever you are." She accepted the challenge of this game. Was it a game?

The darkness became less oppressive when she turned off the lamp.

In the darkness, the radio emitted a single soft click, as if in response to her words.

Chapter 2: First Signal

The morning sunlight entered the room with the same gentle touch as before. The ocean remained hidden behind a white mist which transformed the cottage into a small island that combined ocean sounds with surf noises. Irene was aware of the gentle rhythm, which she now identified as a sound that combined elements from the kettle and clock but maintained its own unique character.

She prepared her tea while keeping the window open by one hand span. The room filled with a gentle breeze to bring in the fresh ocean scent of kelp and wet stone. She tried to dismiss the whisper from last night by telling herself it was either a wind trick or her tired mind creating meaning from radio static.

Even now, the radio drew her attention despite her efforts to ignore it. As if it had risen from sleep, the small table called her attention to the radio, but the red dial she had turned was dark. The old antenna still stretched out from it like a bent shape that resembled a reed growing in shallow water. She placed her mug next to the radio before touching its cool surface. The metal provided her with a sense of comfort. Somehow, there was something more than a radio here. But what was it?

She spoke to the radio because she wanted to hear how her voice sounded, even though there was no one listening. Speaking out loud that way, she realized that she wouldn't know how her voice sounded because there was no way for it to be bounced back to her. Maybe she just wanted to say something out loud. Was she trying to comfort herself?

Her greeting got nothing in return from it. The cottage had taken a deep breath while the sea produced its own deep sound as the briny water hit the rocks. Everything was making a sound except the radio. Silence seemed to be what it preferred at the moment. Was she beginning to think that the radio was alive? Questioning her mental state was not something she wanted to do at this moment, but it almost seemed important.

She moved the dial a quarter of a turn. Only static that sounded like distant rain was its return to her. She turned the dial again, thinking that if she tried hard enough, something would happen again. A brief signal broke into the cottage air before the transmission dissolved into complete silence. Laughing at her own foolishness for expecting something, she turned off the radio as it continued its soft humming sound which was now silent. The voice would select his own time if he truly existed as a real entity. No doubt that there was a presence that determined when and only if the radio would connect with her again.

Not every day at the beach was a warm one, and she put on multiple layers of clothing before she headed down wearing her boots. Fog had created tiny droplets that stuck to her hair and eyelashes that resembled fine lace. In the short time before she walked down to the flat sand, the ocean had already receded in its ocean's rhythm, and it brought her breathing back to normal. Against her face, the air felt fresh and moist, and she breathed it in gratefully.

How could she not speak to the ocean? She spoke with a soft voice. The sand remained dark and solid beneath her feet. An adjacent tidal rock formation was where she listened and expressed her wish to know the reason behind his visit.

She asked him to explain everything. Perhaps that was too much to ask, or perhaps she was being impudent in some way. There was no way to know until she got a response. Would she get a response? After all, she was down here on the beach, not in the cottage. So how would she know if he heard her?

A faint clicking sound emerged from behind her, sounding like a fingernail scraping against glass. Did it come from a gull's beak or a shell moving in a pool of water? She turned to face the fog that held only the faint outline of the cottage buildings. Nothing else was there. All was empty.

She spoke to herself with a mix of amusement and intense thought while saying, "Dinner with ghosts" and "Breakfast with fog." Might as well have some fun while we're down here, she was thinking.

The house had a new atmosphere that felt like a supportive friend who leaned forward to listen. On the table, the radio had a thin ring of moisture from the ocean breeze. A red diamond at the center of the dial now had a faint glow. Something was happening again, and she wasn't sure what it would be.

Irene stopped at the entrance. "Did I forget to turn you off?" No, she didn't think she had forgotten to turn it off. But how could it be on now?

It crackled with more static, followed by a brief period of complete silence, which was short enough for her to be aware of it. It almost sounded like there was some sort of shortwave radio going on.

She took a seat and waited. "I have no idea how to proceed with this because I'm unclear about your nature and your existence. The only thing I know is that last night I had a feeling of being watched by an unseen presence." Throwing down the gauntlet might be the way to get some action.

The static produced a soft sound in response that seemed to indicate someone had released a breath through the radio speaker. Breath?

The voice spoke from a distance as though trying to form words through the fading radio signals. Soft but uncertain, it maintained a steady tone. Was it a voice? Was this all part of a dream?

The skin on her body started to tingle. Without being aware of it, she moved closer to the radio and said her name out loud. "Irene."

The static produced a soft affirmative sound in response. The voice repeated Irene's name with caution as if it were discovering the taste of her words. "Irene."

"Yes." She swallowed. "Yesterday." Being a bit impudent and brave was having an effect.

A long period of silence passed. His thoughts seemed to take a long time to process. He chose to start with the word "Tea" as if he had found a secure starting point. "You have... tea." Surely she was now being observed from somewhere.

She laughed—a quiet, startled sound that felt like a door unlatching. "Yes. I always have tea." How could she be talking to something unseen and totally unrealistic?

The voice gave her a simple command which sounded like a blessing. "Drink."

She followed the instruction because it seemed the normal thing to do. The tea had reached a temperature that wasn't scorching and its warmth passed through her body with the speed of light.

She paused before asking her next question. "How do I have a way to reach you?"

A change occurred in the transmission. The radio signal wavered. "You can reach me through the water," he said while his voice revealed a hint of amusement. Is there something that you want to share with me?"

The air remained silent before he spoke again. "You can reach me through the air. I will... hear."

"Do you have a name?"

"Not yet."

His response was like a delicate space which he protected with care because he treated it like a fragile object that needed both hands to hold it. Names function as both heavy objects and binding elements. The person might keep their name hidden for specific reasons. But what was the reason he wouldn't reveal his name? No way to be sure at this moment, but she hoped that shortly she would get more information.

"You should name me—" She gazed through the window to see the fog clearing and revealing a thin strip of light on the horizon. "Shoreline," she said before feeling embarrassed. "No. That's trying too hard. Maybe just... the Voice." Sounded about right because this voice was coming out of thin air and the ocean.

He repeated the words "The voice," while his amusement was pretty evident from the tone and manner in which the words were being spoken. Amused was he?

The conversation continued for several minutes. It was needed because it seemed this communication almost followed natural weather patterns—unknown and unknowable. But the empty spaces between their words created a sense of shared space instead of isolation.

He took the opportunity to speak first. "What... brings you," he asked with careful words, "to the edge?"

She could have given false reasons for her visit. She could have explained that she visited for vacation or to explore her heritage or because she loved the wind. Instead, she said that she had come to forget and to learn new ways of remembering. Telling someone who existed in thin air one of her secrets surprised even Irene.

The room fell silent as if everyone respected the moment. "What... hurting?"

She shared with him her sister's death during the spring season. "She died this spring. Too young. The hospital equipment continues to play in my mind during my sleepless nights. I continuously attempt to recreate her laughter inside my head. I try, and sometimes I succeed, but not always, and that's very distressing to me."

A deep sound emerged from the Voice indicating he was listening through his entire being. "I'm... sorry." An invisible creature was showing empathy for her when too many in her prior months had failed to do that. She'd missed that.

Without any further thought, she shared with him that her marriage had come to an end through a peaceful process. "The relationship between us remained civil until we lost all connection. I believed I possessed exceptional abilities to stay in relationships. I believed my ability to stay in that relationship was my most valuable skill." Even she was questioning what she had done and what her beliefs had been at that time.

The radio produced an extended wave of static, which felt like his hand finding hers before holding it without applying pressure. "You... came to breathe," he said.

"Yes."

"Yes."

"Good."

Her smile returned while her chest reopened in the same way it had before. "And you?" she asked. "What brings you to the edge?" Didn't she have a right to question back since he was being so curious about her life?

"Edge... is where I live," he said before his words carried the essence of salt and distance and a hint of moonlight for a brief instant. "Between." A small chuckle emerged as if to excuse the enigmatic statement. "It is... a good place to listen."

"We both listen to each other, which seems to be enough for us."

"It is a beginning." He understood.

The stove kettle started making a series of sounds. Irene got up to fill her tea mug before she thought to prepare a second cup as an automatic response. She placed the additional mug on the table, and heat rose from it like a peaceful spirit.

Warily, she checked the clock before she blinked. The current time was midday. "You sound like someone's uncle," she teased. "Or someone's... therapist."

"I'd position a chair near the window if I had access to one."

His simple joke brought her back to reality. She spread butter on a slice of bread before taking a bite while realizing her appetite had returned like a bird returning to its nest. The radio continued to sound its presence through irregular transmissions which brought her the same comfort as having a close friend. He spoke her name after a pause.

"When fog lifts, go... to market. Buy apples. Speak to the woman who laughs with her whole face. She will... know your aunt." A spirit wasn't only looking after her health, it was advising her about people in the town who knew her aunt.

Irene furrowed her brow. "Mrs. Dobbins?"

"Yes," he said, sure this time.

"How do you—" She stopped. She chose to avoid asking for his qualifications because she wanted to preserve the mystery. "All right. I'll visit the market this afternoon when the fog disappears."

"The weather will clear," he said with great assurance and with the same confidence that someone who studied weather patterns until they became his native language would use.

"They will ask how long you will stay. Answer, 'Long enough.' It will be... the right size of truth."

The advice he gave her made her laugh because it brought out a tender feeling in her. "Long enough," she repeated while she practiced the way the words sounded. "You're very good at this." Did he have practice, she wondered, but she didn't ask. Had he spoken to her aunt?

"Listening," he said, and she knew his smile had returned. "And... staying with people, while they find words."

"You mean... staying with me," she said, not as a demand but as a recognition.

"Yes."

The river of light expanded across the horizon while the fog transformed into a thin gauze before it completely disappeared. The sea revealed its full beauty to the world at two o'clock in the afternoon. Irene put on her coat before tying her scarf around her neck. Then she paused at the cottage entrance and turned to look back.

"Will you—will you be here when I come back?" How could she ask a spirit where they would be? But she wanted him to be there when she returned. Yes, a connection was forming.

"I am... tide," he said, affectionately. "I return." Somehow he's a part of the ocean? So many things she wanted to know, so many questions she wanted to ask, but all of that would have to wait if he were willing to reveal any of it.

She stepped into the bright new world which rewarded her with vibrant colors that replaced the monochromatic view of the morning. The village nestled in a natural depression between the coastline and the harbor and its roofs resembled folded paper boats. Quaint, most people would say when trying to describe it. For sure it was quaint.

The market area had been planned with a practical design, organizing vegetable displays, faded flags, and friendly local chatter that avoided any invasive behavior. It was quite an insular community, but it was friendly and open, and different for her now.

Mrs. Dobbins' face turned into a complete vision of happiness as she laughed; Irene immediately recognized the description. The woman reached for an apple before Irene asked while she used her apron to clean the fruit until it became a small sun. How could she have known what Irene wanted if Irene hadn't told her?

"You'd be the niece who lives at the Morrow cottage," she said with a broad smile that didn't hide any intentions. "I see your aunt in your eyes. She listened to ships as if they were neighbors who lived nearby." The woman knew her aunt as he had said she would.

"My aunt and her radio," Irene said, feeling a surge of affection when she thought about it. "She believed the airwaves brought companionship to anyone who learned to listen to them."

Mrs. Dobbins nodded. "Still does. You just have to sit still long enough to be found." The secret was sitting and listening until you were found?

Irene bought apples and an unnecessary loaf of bread while she expressed excessive gratitude to the people she met. The woman told Irene to come to the harvest supper in two weeks, bringing only herself and the shawl she wore. "The library rota wants your participation on Thursdays," according to Mrs. Dobbins. Irene left with a paper bag with food while her body developed an unusual fizzy sensation that felt like laughter before she understood the joke. Something was happening, and it seemed to be good.

The sunlight reached honey-like tones when she arrived at the top of the cottage path. Once there, she used the top step to clean her boots before putting down the bag that rested on her hip. At that moment she felt "it" as she was filled with the comfort of entering a door that swung open easily. It wasn't the door, but what waited for her inside.

"I went," she said while letting the words drift toward the radio as she arranged the apples in a bowl. "Mrs. Dobbins remembers my aunt's shawl and her specific tea choices. The library wants me to work on Thursdays unless I protest loudly and the harvest supper will take place two weeks from now."

"Good."

Irene took her seat at the table and picked up an apple to eat as she reflected on the distance between her past and present. The overly ripe apple became a complete mess after she finished eating it. Searching for a napkin to wipe off splashes of juice, she laughed.

Wasn't it time for him to share information in exchange for sharing her knowledge?

"Anything at all. Trade me a fact for a fact."

The static changed as he started to prepare his words. "I used to study ocean currents by studying how oil droplets on water surfaces created patterns which resembled handwritten messages." A soft pause. "I don't understand why this experience feels like the appropriate gift to give."

Her reply was, "Because it's beautiful and because you've seen beyond the dangers and distances to understand the world's attempt at communication. "It's beautiful," she said, as tears stung her eyes. "Because it means you saw more than danger and distance. You saw the world trying to talk."

Another pause. She stood at the window while he studied the ocean patterns which resembled handwritten messages that continued to arrive without end. She wanted to ask his name again but she chose not to. Maybe it was too soon.

"My fact," she said instead. "My sister asked me to continue preparing regular meals during her final days of life. The meals should remain ordinary instead of becoming memorial feasts or sacred rituals. They should be pasta on Tuesdays and soup during rainy days. She said to avoid turning grief into the main dish on our table. I promised." Irene used her wrist to wipe away the apple juice which had dried into a sticky and sweet residue. "I'm out of practice."

He spoke softly about Thursday soup and market day apples as if he were creating a schedule. "Thursday... soup," he said quietly, as if setting a calendar note in the sky. "And on market day, apples."

The two of them kept their position through the entire transition from afternoon gold to evening blue until they reached evening. She asked him about the window latch and the closet moisture problem. He provided her with local knowledge that the house seemed to recall from memory. He asked her about her daily activities while she fought back tears until he maintained complete silence until her emotions subsided.

She announced her plan to visit the library on Thursday when the first star emerged through the evening sky. "I'll go to the library on Thursday."

"Yes."

She decided to bring a store-bought pie to the harvest supper where she'd pretend it was homemade. "Everyone... does," he said, and she knew he was smiling again.

Next, she turned on the lamp before standing up. The room had a peaceful atmosphere that supported her. The ocean outside reflected back the cleaned and organized version of the day. It had been a special day. She prepared her bed before returning to the table while keeping her hand on the radio as if to bless it.

"I'll be here tomorrow," she said. "If you are."

"I am tide," he reminded her. "I return."

She hesitated before introducing a bit of playfulness into her voice. "Therapist," she teased. "From beyond."

"Guide," he countered, amused. "From between."

They said goodnight. The red dial dimmed but did not go entirely dark. She kept the window slightly open to let the sea touch the furniture while she slept.

This evening, there was the same feeling of being protected by an unseen presence that didn't observe her. The hospital environment had lacked this feeling of protection. The whole experience felt like having someone guide her around the edge of a cliff while they trusted her to decide when to stop and when to continue.

Resting her head back while thinking about Mrs. Dobbins' joyful face and the market flags and the library records with their organized Thursday schedule was another pleasure as was the pie she would pass off as homemade. She visualized the radio's steady red light and the unidentified name of the man who spoke as if he listened to people as his life's purpose. Through it all she envisioned herself living among people who treated her as a regular member of their community. The first wave of sleep arrived before it disappeared again before returning for a second time.

The radio sounded a single deliberate click before she fell asleep as if someone outside had adjusted the dial by one inch before releasing it.

Chapter 3: Shared Solitude

The village came to life slowly, as if unsure it wanted to be awakened. Irene parked her car near the pier and stepped out into the crisp air. It felt good. The air, however, smelled of salt mixed with diesel from the small boats already rocking at anchor. A handful of fishermen with their dogs moved along the dock, their voices carrying low and familiar over the water. The day had begun, and she was glad to be there.

Keeping her head down against the occasional gusts of wind, she walked toward the market. People looked at her with polite interest—she was still new, even though the cottage where she was staying wasn't. A few nodded; others flashed small smiles. One woman behind the counter at the bakery recognized her immediately. It was a pleasant relief.

"You're the niece," she said, dusting her hands on her apron. "She used to send me jars of preserves every winter. You staying through the season?"

Irene nodded. "That's the plan." Even though she didn't know if she was staying through the season, Irene decided to put the question to rest. Who would know what she was going to do, even she wasn't sure at this point. But through the season sounded like a good choice.

"Well, the wind will have its say about that," the woman laughed. "It gets into your bones if you let it." The townspeople sure knew their weather.

Irene smiled faintly, took her loaf of bread, and made her way back to the car.

The drive home was quiet except for the sound of the tires on the slippery wet road. She tried not to think about the Voice. But every time she caught the shape of the sea out of the corner of her eye, she felt the question pressing closer—who was he, really? And why did it matter so much that she didn't want to stop hearing him? Questions kept coming to her, and as soon as they came, she attempted to dismiss them from her mind. Time would tell who he was, where he came from, and the reason he had come to her. What was the reason? Was he some kind of savior, or had he been sent by her aunt? Maybe her sister was the one.

When she returned, the house was cool. After she set her groceries on the counter, she took off her coat and glanced toward the table where the radio sat, still and unlit. The silence seemed expectant. Actually, it wasn't expected because she had hoped he might be there even now. But he wasn't.

She told herself she wouldn't touch it. She had real things to do—laundry, sorting through the boxes her aunt had left, maybe a walk before the rain came in. But as she reached for a towel, her eyes drifted back. No response yet.

By midafternoon, she gave up pretending.

She crossed the room, sat down, and ran her fingers over the familiar dials. "If you're there," she said softly, "I could use the company." It was like reaching out into a void and not knowing if anything would be there.

At first, nothing. Then, there was the thin hiss of static; slowly, a faint rhythm again—soft, almost polite, like someone clearing his throat before speaking.

"You came back." Her own voice almost shocked her because she wasn't thinking she would say anything, but it just blurted out.

Irene exhaled a breath she hadn't realized she was holding. "I wasn't sure you'd answer." Was she sounding a bit pathetic?

"I wasn't sure you'd call," he replied. He, on the other hand, seemed quite self-assured.

His tone was as it had been before—calm, unhurried. There was something deeply human in it, something that quieted the part of her that still wanted to call this impossible. "Impossible" certainly was the word, and if she revealed it to anyone, they would wonder if she were suffering from some illness.

"I went into town," she said. "Everyone seems to know who my aunt was."

"She made herself known. She didn't keep to herself the way you do." How was he questioning what she was doing? She'd only been there a short time. Already he seemed to know more about her than what he had learned here in the cottage.

Irene smiled. "You make that sound like a criticism."

"It's not," he said. "You listen before you speak. That's a kind of kindness."

No one had ever said that to her before. Not her husband, not the friends who had drifted away after her sister's death. She'd always been the quiet one—not shy, just careful. Hearing someone notice it without judgment unsettled her in the best way.

"You must have a lot of time for listening," she said.

"I do. But it's different when someone listens back." Were there others that he was speaking to? She wondered.

The simplicity of it stilled her. She rested her hand lightly on the side of the radio, the way one might on a friend's shoulder.

"I used to hate quiet," she admitted. "It reminded me of hospitals—the kind of silence that's heavy because you're waiting for bad news." Those days in the hospital came back in unpleasant spurts, and she tried to push them away. They weren't pleasant memories. In fact, they were quite painful.

"And now?" he asked.

"Now it's different. It's not empty here."

He didn't speak for a while. When he did, the sound came slower, as if he were turning the thought over carefully. "You're learning to live with the space. That's not easy."

Irene looked out the window. The tide was rising again, and the surf had turned rougher, whitecaps forming under a sky the color of pewter. Yes, the weather was turning, and she wondered what he might say about that.

"You talk like someone who's done it," she said.

"I've had time to think about what it means to stay," he said.

She frowned. "Stay?" What did he mean by saying "stay?"

There was a pause, then a quiet shift in tone—not somber, but honest. "I couldn't leave when I was supposed to. I think your aunt understood that. She didn't try to fix it." Her aunt spoke to him, too, over the radio. Now she wanted to know more.

A chill went through her, though the air in the room hadn't changed. "You mean..."

"I mean, I'm not like the others you talk to," he said gently. "But I'm not here to frighten you." Like the others? What others was he referring to?

He said it with such steady certainty that, to her surprise, she wasn't frightened. She felt only a wave of compassion—for him, for herself, for every soul caught somewhere between past and possibility. There must have been others, and he was letting her know she wasn't alone.

"You sound very alive," she said quietly.

"Maybe that's what happens when someone finally listens." Could it be that he also needed someone to listen to him?

The words settled between them, unforced. The static softened until it became the faintest hum, like the sea whispering through walls.

They spoke for a long time after that—not about loss, not about death, but about small things. What she'd seen on the drive. How the air changed before rain. The old cat that sometimes wandered near the porch. He asked questions, simple ones, the kind people ask when they want to know who you are, not just what you've done.

At one point, she laughed—really laughed—and the sound startled her. After all, laughing at what must only be referred to as a ghost was a bit unusual.

"I haven't done that in a while," she said. It felt good to laugh.

"It suits you," he replied.

The radio made a soft click, as if it had sighed in agreement. The air felt lighter. She sat there until the light outside dimmed to blue, until her reflection was all she could see in the window.

"I should go," she said reluctantly. "I still have to eat something."

"Then eat," he said. "But don't stop listening. Not to me—to the world again." Ghost therapy was just what she needed now.

She smiled. "That sounds like something my sister would've said."

"Then maybe she taught us both."

The hum faded, soft and complete, like a breath drawn in and held.

Irene stayed a few minutes longer, her hand still resting on the radio. Then she turned it off and went to the window. Outside, the sea moved with quiet rhythm, and she could swear the wind carried something warm through the cracks—not words, but a feeling. There was a presence undoubtedly, and it was him, even if the radio wasn't on.

Not loneliness anymore. Something close to comfort.

Chapter 4:
Between Worlds

The weather settled for a few days. Mornings came bright and cool, and the water near the rocks smoothed out between tides. Irene adjusted to a routine that had nothing remarkable in it: tea, a walk along the lane, some time with the boxes in the back room, and a few pages from her aunt's journal. She went to the village twice—bread from the bakery, apples from Mrs. Dobbins, a small jar of honey someone had left on a table with a handwritten price. People remembered her aunt. They took their time in conversation. No one pried. Everything seemed to be falling into place as she became adjusted to the new rhythm of the cottage, the sea, and the community.

Inside the cottage, she opened windows earlier and left them open longer. Sea air filled the entire space and it held with it a promise of something more. The cottage began to feel lived in rather than just visited. She repaired a sticky latch, wiped the dust from the bookshelf, and stacked the radio notebooks in a neat pile.

The radio stayed where it always sat, but she no longer approached it with caution. Eager anticipation had replaced the initial caution she had felt. She turned the dials when she wanted to talk and let the silence sit when she didn't. The quiet didn't bother her anymore. It felt natural.

On the fourth morning, she sat at the table with the window cracked an inch and her tea cooling. The radio was off. She didn't reach for it because she knew that if he wanted to contact her, she didn't have to do anything. The room had a plain calm: the tick of the clock, a gull somewhere above the roofline, the steady push and pull of the sea. She noticed how her shoulders felt—less tight and more natural in their lift and fall and it surprised her. She had not decided anything. The change had just arrived. It was all so natural, and everything seemed to be as it should be.

Later, she put on a sweater and went out to the headland. The grass there was stiff and short from wind, and the path to the cliff edge was familiar after only a week. She stood where the land dropped away and watched the water move in long, even strokes. She wasn't counting waves. She wasn't thinking about grief. Then she turned back when the wind found a colder edge.

When she opened the door, the radio clicked once, not loud—just a clean sound like a switch making contact. She set the bag of apples on the counter and waited. Nothing. She smiled to herself and reached for the sink tap. He's waiting, she thought. So he must be in some way observing me.

Finally, he said, "You're back," his voice steady and close.

"I am." She dried her hands on a dish towel. "I brought apples."

"Good choice," he said. "They keep you honest about hunger." Did hunger have honesty? Maybe he meant something else that she would have to think about.

"That sounds like something my doctor would say."

"I mean it the simple way," he said. "They remind you to eat." Not only was he advising her, but he was also encouraging her.

She sat, pulled an apple from the bag, and cut it into quarters. The knife made a firm sound on the board. When she ate the first slice, the sweetness surprised her.

"How are you today?" she asked.

"Listening," he said. "You were standing by the cliff."

"Only for a few minutes."

"Long enough," he said.

She glanced at the window. "You always know where I am?"

"I know how a room feels without you in it," he answered, not dramatic, just factual. "And how it feels when you come back." What was he telling her now? It seemed as though he was saying the room wasn't complete without her, and he felt a sense of loss.

She didn't argue. It was the kind of statement that would have bothered her a week ago. Now it slid into place, the way the latch had after she sanded the frame.

"I've been reading your notebooks," she said, nodding toward the little stack. "You logged dates and weather. Notes about 'northbound traffic' and 'clear sky, long skip.' I had to look that up." She had to admit that she knew little to nothing about shipping, but her aunt's notes had helped to fill in the blanks in her knowledge base.

"Your aunt enjoyed the way signals jump on certain nights," he said. "She liked learning what the air could carry."

"She wrote your initials once," Irene said. "Only once. 'Spoke with E. Familiar route tonight.'"

"Ah," he said, and then nothing for a breath. "She gave me privacy."

"Do you want me to use your name?" Irene asked. Has anyone ever asked a spirit for permission to call them by name?

"I don't need it," he said. "If you do, choose the one that lets you speak to me without effort." So he was saying that she could call him any name she wished?

"That feels like a lot of responsibility." But she wanted a name for him.

"You've carried more."

She finished the apple and set the knife aside. "I went to the library notice board," she said. "I put my name down for Thursday afternoons."

"Good," he said. "Three o'clock is busy at first, then quiet after the school crowd leaves." He even knew what was happening at the library on specific days and even with schoolchildren.

"You know the schedule?"

"Some things don't change much," he said, and she could hear the slight lilt in his voice.

"People have started asking how long I'm staying," she said.

"What do you tell them?"

"'Long enough.'"

"That fits," he said. Again, he was reassuring her that he knew she was going to make the right decisions for herself.

She stood to make tea. The kettle took its time; she didn't rush it. While she waited, she sorted the morning mail: a flyer for the harvest supper, a bill, a postcard with a picture of the lighthouse from a shop that had just opened for the season. She propped the postcard on the mantle and turned back to the stove.

"Tell me about your sister," he said, as if they'd agreed on this already. When had she indicated that she might want to talk to him about her sister?

Irene set the cups on the table. "She was brighter than me," she said. "Not louder. Just—she took in less and gave out more. She liked to make lists and then ignore them. She laughed a lot. She hated needles."

He didn't interrupt.

"I kept a notebook during the last months," Irene went on. "It's in the bedroom drawer. I wrote down questions for the doctors. Who to call. What time to give the next dose. I wrote what she wanted to eat even when she couldn't. Occasionally, I read it now to remember that we did the best we could."

"You did," he said. Again, quiet reassurance.

"It doesn't always feel like that," she admitted. There had been times when she questioned, but now he was telling her she had done everything she could.

"I know," he said. "But it's still true."

The tea steamed between them. She wrapped her hands around the cup and let the heat work its way in. The radio hummed not as a sound but as presence. She felt watched over without being watched. It felt good.

"I think I stopped trying to make sense of this," she said after a while. "Not just you. The order of things."

"That helps," he said. "Sense can come later. Sometimes it never comes. You can still live well."

"I used to track my days like rows on a spreadsheet," she said, almost amused. "Meetings. Goals. Benchmarks. Now I look at the weather report and decide about laundry." It seemed so simple now that she almost laughed at its absurdity.

"That's still planning," he said. "It's just closer to the ground."

She smiled. "You make these small statements that feel like they've been sitting in a drawer for me to find."

"I'm only saying what fits," he said.

They didn't talk for a few minutes. The cottage held them both. A breeze moved the curtain and carried salt air into the room. She listened to the ordinary sounds—the soft tap of the cord against the window frame, the tick of the cooling kettle, a car somewhere far down the lane. It was all enough.

"I saw Daniel in town," she said, her voice even. "He was fixing the loose board on the library steps."

"He's good with what needs doing," the voice said. "He learns by looking."

"You sound like you approve."

"I like people who mend things," he answered. Was he mending her now?

She didn't say more. She didn't need to. Something unclenched inside her. It wasn't permission. It was clearance, like the white flag the harbor master raised when the channel was open.

"When the harvest supper comes," he said, "bring bread. Still warm, if you can. It will place you at the table without anyone thinking about it."

"That's very specific," she said. Incredibly, he knew more than she ever thought. It was about the town and all the people in it.

"It works," he said.

She looked at the radio. "Were you always like this—practical?"

"I liked problems I could carry in my hands," he said. "A loose line. A map that needed reading. A person who needed time to express their thoughts."

Irene nodded. "You were good at your work."

"I learned to be," he said. "The sea teaches by repetition."

She let out a breath that was almost a laugh. "You're doing it again."

"What?"

"Giving me something I can use. In one sentence."

"Keep the kettle full," he said. "It solves more than it seems."

"Fine," she said. "I'll write that down." They were having a verbal dance that was charming.

Evening came on without color—just a soft thinning of light. She lit the lamp and left it low. The radio's small red lens didn't glow; it didn't have to. She felt his attention where she would have felt a person standing at the doorway.

"I think I'm done asking how you're here," she said. "It isn't helping."

"No," he said. "You don't need it."

"What do I need?"

"Company," he said. "And a next small thing to do."

She considered that. "Tomorrow I'll take the rug outside and beat the sand from it," she said. "I'll do the windows. I'll sign up for the Thursday rota."

"That's enough," he said.

She stood to wash the cups. The warm water ran clear over her hands. She dried the dishes and put them back in the same place each time. When she returned to the table, she left the radio as it was. No click, no adjustment. It stayed quiet and near.

"I'm going to sleep," she said.

"Goodnight," he said. "Leave the window open an inch. The house breathes better that way."

She did. In bed, she lay on her side and watched the rectangle of pale light on the wall. She didn't wait for a sign. She didn't whisper for one. The sea sounded like itself. Her heartbeat slowed to meet it.

Before she drifted off, she noticed something modest and real: for the first time since she'd come to the cottage, she wasn't measuring the distance between what she believed and what she felt. She had let the question go. She had made space for two truths to sit in the same room.

When sleep came, it was simple. The window was open an inch. The house held steady. Somewhere in the wiring or the air, the frequency stayed where it was, ready for morning.

Chapter 5: The Village Festival

The morning of the festival started with a steady north wind and a clear sky. Banners went up across the village green by nine, and the bakery set out trays of freshly made hand pies that steamed in the cold air. Irene watched from the edge of the square for a minute before stepping in. How could she not be part of this since staying at the cottage had connected her so to this community? She had walked down to the green early on purpose, hoping to find her footing before the crowd thickened. Would it work, or would she feel like a third wheel? No, the people had already shown their friendly attitude toward her and her aunt.

Mrs. Dobbins waved from the produce table. "You came. Good. We need another pair of hands." Asking to join in was as much of an invitation as anyone could want, and Irene gladly accepted.

Slipping behind the table she started bagging apples. People paid in exact change or small bills, talking about the weather and the year's catch. A boy with a gap in his front teeth asked if he could pick the spotted ones for a discount. "Two for one," she said, and the boy ran off grinning, holding his paper bag like a prize. Already she was making deals for the stand, and no one objected.

By late morning the square filled. A trio of high schoolers tuned a guitar, then changed their minds and tuned again. Someone rolled a cider barrel into the shade. Children ran between the tables holding sticks of special cotton candy spun sugar that turned their tongues blue. How many mothers were going to think they had a sick child on their hands that day?

Ordinarily, it was the kind of scene she used to avoid—the noise, the brush of shoulders, the need to speak without a script—but she found herself settling into it. The work was simple. The small talk stayed small. It was enough. Could it have been any easier? She didn't think so. Perhaps the Voice knew, and he had guided her to somewhere she had always wanted to be but never knew that.

"Take a break," Mrs. Dobbins said, handing her a mug. "Hot cider. Sweet enough to keep you on your feet."

Irene stepped to the edge of the green and sipped. The heat moved through her slowly. On the far side of the square, a man on a ladder was adjusting a string of lights that kept sagging in the middle. The ladder wobbled. A second man—tall, dark jacket—reached up and steadied it with one arm while he talked to a woman passing with a tray of rolls. The movement was easy, unhurried. Everything seemed perfect.

"Daniel," someone said behind her. "He's got a hand in everything and doesn't make a fuss."

Irene turned. The speaker had already moved on, but the name stuck. Here was that fellow Daniel fixing things again.

She finished her cider and returned to the table. A lull set in around noon, as it often does when people go home for lunch, and she used the quiet to stack new baskets of fruit. The wind picked up enough to tug at the corners of the banners. From somewhere overhead came a soft hum—lights warming, a speaker testing. Announcements were probably going to be made, and she wondered what they might be.

Then the familiar click sounded in her head, not loud, more like a change in air pressure. She didn't look around for the radio. She didn't need to because she had the feeling that he was always wherever she was, and it wasn't confined to the cottage any longer.

"You're doing fine," the Voice said, low and easy, like a reminder she'd written to herself. It wasn't through a speaker or a wire. It was a presence—clear as a hand on a shoulder without the weight. Again, she had that sensation of being watched in a good way and cared for at the same time.

She kept her eyes on the apples. "I was waiting to see if you'd show up," she said in the quiet space between conversations.

"I said I would," he replied. "How's the crowd?"

"Friendly. Loud in places. Manageable."

"You'll like the evening best," he said. "Lanterns. Songs you can sing without thinking."

She nodded once. "I can stay for that." Information was being exchanged, and bargains were being struck. She liked all of them.

A woman approached with a list and a purposeful walk. "You're the niece," she said, out of breath. "Can you run the pie table for half an hour? Our usual helper sprained her ankle."

"I can do that," Irene said. First apples, now pies. The community was including her as one of its own.

The pie table sat near the corner where the lights crossed the street. She took her station, lined up plates, and started cutting clean slices. People asked what was in each one. She told them without reaching for labels. Blueberry. Apple. Pumpkin with too much clove, which some people liked. She kept her hands busy and her answers short. Customers were very pleased with the selection and with her help.

"Two slices of apple, please," a man said. He set down a few bills and waited while she lifted the pieces onto paper plates. When she looked up, she met the kind of face that makes you change your posture—open, steady, slightly amused. He wore the same dark jacket she'd seen near the ladder.

"Thank you," he said, taking the plates. "You're new here."

"New-ish," she said. "I'm at the Morrow cottage."

"Ah," he said, recognition settling in. "I helped fix the porch rail last winter when your aunt was under the weather. Good wood, bad nails." He had a sense of humor, and she liked that.

"She always did the small repairs herself," Irene said. "But she wrote lists for the rest." She heard her own voice and felt a small, unexpected lift in her chest. It was easier to say now.

"I'm Daniel," he said, switching one plate to his other hand so he could offer a free one.

"Irene," she said.

He nodded. "Welcome back." Had he known her when she came as a young girl to visit? She didn't remember him.

She wanted to ask what he meant by "back," but the line behind him had grown. He stepped aside without making it awkward. Nearby, someone started a tune people recognized by the second bar. Feet tapped. A child spun in a circle and fell down laughing.

"Steady," the Voice said, quiet at her shoulder. "You're doing exactly what you came here to do."

"Which is what?" she asked silently, moving the knife through pumpkin that didn't want to cooperate.

"Be here," he said. "The rest will sort itself."

By late afternoon, the sky took on a clear, pale color that made the edges of things look clean—the church steeple, the clapboard storefronts, and the gulls turning into the wind and holding there for a beat before deciding to move on. Gulls floated on air and moved with the invisible current. And Irene was feeling like that, too. Volunteers strung more lights. A makeshift stage went up on a flatbed truck. People pulled sweaters from bags and handed them across to one another without asking whose was whose. Community.

Daniel returned with a stack of empty plates. "Need a hand?" he asked.

"Please," she said, and shifted to make room.

They worked without much talk. He slid slices onto plates while she took money and made change. The movement found a rhythm almost immediately. When the last pie went, they both looked at the clean table at the same time and laughed once, softly, like people who had finished a task that wasn't complicated but still felt satisfying to complete.

"Do you want to walk a bit?" he asked. "I need to check the lights before dusk."

"All right," she said.

They walked along the edge of the green. He tested each connection with a small twist of his fingers, not rough, not showy. She kept pace without trying. At the far end, a group of teenagers were arguing about whether a particular song was too old to play. Daniel smiled without joining in. What a wonderful disposition he had, she thought.

"You didn't live here originally?" he asked as they headed back.

"Childhood summers," she said. "Then only visits. Now... we'll see."

"That's a fair answer," he said. "This place has a way of asking without waiting for your reply."

She glanced toward the headland. The line of the path to the cottage showed as a notch against the sky. For a moment her breath shortened, just slightly, as if she'd climbed more steps than she had.

"I'll walk you partway later," Daniel said, like an offer made to the air, not a pressure. "It gets dark fast once the sun drops."

"I'll be fine," she said, then added, "Thank you."

He tipped his head once. "I'll look for you near the music."

Dusk slid in quietly. Lanterns came alive in a slow wave as someone connected the final run. The first song started without introduction. People didn't face the stage like an audience; they stayed in their clusters, talking, singing along when they knew the words, clapping when the drummer asked too nicely to ignore.

Irene stood where she was and let the sound settle around her. The Voice was there, not loud, not even separate, more like a line that ran under the music, warm and steady.

"You're safe," he said, and the assurance landed in a plain, practical way, like someone checking a lock.

She drew a breath and let it out. "Stay a little," she thought.

"I will," he said. "But not right at your shoulder. You don't need that tonight."

She nodded once. A few minutes later, Daniel appeared with two paper cups. He handed one to her without comment. The cider had gone lukewarm, but the cinnamon was strong. They stood together, watching a boy play a solo that was mostly confidence. When the song ended, the applause was genuine.

"Are you up for the walk?" he asked after a while, tipping his head toward the dark rise of the lane.

"Yes," she said. "I think I am." Everything was so natural, and together they seemed to have something she couldn't quite put her finger on.

They left the square by the side street to avoid the knots of people saying long goodnights. The lane climbed in a gradual curve, the gravel firm underfoot. Wind pushed from the water dried the sweat on the back of her neck. Neither of them spoke until the turn where the path to the cottage began. Daniel stopped and looked toward the thin light in her front window.

"You've got a good place there," he said. "It sits right. Not all houses do."

"I'm starting to see that," she said.

"Goodnight, Irene"

"Goodnight."

He stood there until she reached the porch, then lifted a hand in a goodnight gesture and went back down the lane.

Inside, the cottage held the day's heat low and even. Irene set her cup in the sink and turned toward the table. The radio sat as it always did. No glow. No sound. She didn't touch it. She didn't need to. The house felt full in the right way—work done, faces learned, names beginning to attach to them.

"Thank you," she said into the room, not raising her voice.

The answer came like it always did when she'd made a step on her own—quiet, certain, without ceremony. "You're welcome," he said. "Rest."

She locked the door, left the window open a few inches, and sat on the edge of the bed to unlace her boots. Her hands were sticky with sugar and cinnamon. Her feet hurt. None of it felt like a problem. She lay back and listened. Music from the green reached her in a thin thread, carried by the wind. Under it came the steady sound of the sea.

She slept as soon as her eyes closed. Nothing dramatic happened. The house settled. The tide turned. Morning would bring dishes, a broom, a walk to the notice board to confirm Thursday's hours. For now, the world kept its shape, and she kept hers inside it.

Chapter 6: Longing Without Touch

The following days brought pleasant weather, which included bright mornings and dry winds that carried sea salt and faint notes of rope. Irene followed a new daily pattern, which required no explanation because she worked at the library on Thursdays and bought groceries on Tuesdays and kept her windows open until the air became cold.

Stability was found in regularity. Her life had taken on a new type of regular actions that were comfortable and perfectly suited her. She spent her evening hours listening to the radio while sipping tea. The two of them took turns starting their conversations. The pattern between them developed into a natural habit, that emerged from their daily conversations. Regular conversations with the spirit. Who knows what people would have thought, but she found it totally satisfying.

Daniel visited the house for some specific reasons; the porch light needed a replacement bulb. The path leading to the cottage also needed something: a specific grade adjustment, which he could complete using two shovels and a level. His visits became longer only when she specifically asked him to stay. His voice was always at a low pitch without any intention of being secretive. The person he was had a talent for selecting spaces instead of dominating them.

He arrived at her door with a paper bag in his hand. "I brought apples from the trees near the school," he explained. "The apples have a short shelf life before they become spoiled." Well, apples that were going to ripen so quickly led to another discussion.

She took the bag from him before putting it on the kitchen counter. "You want to force me into baking pies, don't you?" Being a bit coquette-ish and joking seems so good now.

"Not force," he said. "Encourage."

The two of them shared a laugh because they had chosen to like each other and were waiting for a solid reason to do so. He inspected the window latch she had fixed before giving it a brief nod of approval. He touched the doorframe with his fingers before he left as if he were counting something. She watched his hand move along the wood, which brought her a sense of comfort.

The wind direction changed that evening. The house responded with a new sound, that consisted of soft breathing instead of creaking. Irene turned off the lamp to listen in the darkness. A click emitted from the radio, sounding like a small switch.

"I'm here," he said.

"I know," she answered without any surprise while maintaining her complete attention.

"How was your day?"

"Useful," she said. "Windows, the path, apples. A man visited the square to sharpen knives while operating a foot pedal, and he discussed blade characteristics as if they were human personalities."

"I remember him," the Voice said. "He becomes silent when he works with thin blades. He shows respect for established boundaries."

Irene smiled in the darkness of the room. "That's exactly it."

The two spent time in complete silence. Her breathing pattern returned to normal. The ocean waves produced a constant sound that resembled human footsteps when someone walks through a familiar hallway. Things were beginning to fall into place so naturally that she never questioned anything now.

He suggested she should bake the pie for tomorrow while bringing half to Mrs. Dobbins and storing two slices in the freezer even if she forgot about them.

"Why?"

"Because it will transform the cottage into a space where something has been created," he explained. "The way a room feels changes when this happens."

"Does it really make such a difference?" Often he would say things that she didn't quite understand, but she knew that he knew she soon would realize the importance of what he said.

"It makes enough of a difference."

She could have started an argument at that moment. She didn't. "All right," she said. "Tomorrow."

The next morning, she began making the pie dough on the kitchen table while keeping the radio notebooks away from the flour area. The apples were firm and resisted the knife. She worked without music while the peeler produced its slow scraping sound and the knife made its cutting noise. The kitchen temperature increased. The air carried a strong scent of cinnamon. She lost track of time during her work.

The baked pies had a lovely uniform crust browning, but the oven heat created darker spots at their edges. After baking, she knew that the pies needed to rest, and so she opened the window. The wind raised the curtain before it brushed her face before continuing its path. An entire minute was spent without thinking about anything which brought her a better state of mind than she had experienced in several weeks. After finishing the baking she told him he had been correct about the room transformation.

"I know," he said, a little pleased.

"Don't get smug."

"I won't," he said, and she knew he was smiling.

One pie she brought to the village during the afternoon hours. The villagers made way for her without any words because they had already accepted her as one of their own. Mrs. Dobbins took the pie and said it would receive "proper gratitude" and she asked Irene to watch the library desk on Thursday again while she took her grandson to the dentist. Irene agreed to help without thinking about any possible reasons to refuse. After all, isn't that what neighbors do for each other? And hadn't she agreed to mind the library desk anyway?

Daniel greeted her when she returned home from her errand. "You baked pastry," he said as he knew the scent in the air and saw the empty pie pan.

"I baked a pie," she said. "I'm not ready to say I'm skilled at pastry making." She had tried it, and it turned out very well. Trying new things was getting to be more natural for her.

He walked with her until they reached the lane before he left without making any plans. Somehow, he handled possibilities by keeping doors open while staying out of their way.

The evenings brought a subtle change to her life that wasn't intense. Between them, the space grew warm, crafting a closeness that needed no effort. While reading, the pages of her book stayed flat. She slept better during the night. On the table, she put her cup down and then somehow it was adjusted in the saucer. She ignored the radio during that time.

"Was that you?" she said later.

"Yes," he answered.

"You shouldn't move things."

"I know," he said. "It helps sometimes, to be real enough to push back."

She wondered about the heavy nature of grief and how memories could create pressure. There was a realization of a need. She recognized the need to prove her existence through the way her breath created window fog and the way a cup aligned perfectly. But the cup had done it with a little assistance, hadn't it?

Opening up a bit more to the Voice, she shared bits and pieces about Daniel through casual conversations instead of telling a complete story. The way he checked his work and his ability to listen to children in the square when they asked so many questions and his practice of not filling all silences.

"He sounds like someone who will look up when you enter a room," the Voice said.

"He does," she said. "It's nothing big. It feels big anyway."

"That's how you know it's yours," he said.

She drifted into sleep quickly that evening before she felt a sensation of a gentle hand resting near her body but not making contact. The experience brought no fear to her as the presence of another person filled the space. She went back to sleep without adjusting her pillow.

The following day she focused on performing minor maintenance jobs. Daniel brought his toolbox with him when he reached her doorstep. "Your porch rail needs additional support because it wobbles?" he asked.

"You'll hold, I'll drill."

They worked together, and he explained. "We can install a support beam that'll stabilize the structure." The cottage did need a bit of help with some of its features, and Daniel certainly was the person to do it.

"We'll work as a team." The wooden debris piled up at the base of the staircase, as he made the measurements with precision without ever saying the words. He showed her that the better angle for support would result from a shallower cut. Afterward, she tested the rail by placing her full body weight on it, and the structure supported her without any issues. It worked out well, and he did a fine job. But what else would she have expected from him?

"Better," he said.

"Better," she agreed.

He left without saying anything about the next time they would be together. The way he raised his hand brought her more satisfaction than she had anticipated. It wasn't so much a goodbye gesture as an "I'll be here" gesture.

Entering the house, she began to clean her hands before stopping at the dining table. Work isn't always clean, and her hands had picked up quite a bit of dust and dirt. The radio stayed at its regular position on the table and she left it alone. She didn't need to touch it. The room now had a new equilibrium through completed work and cooling tea and floor illumination.

It had been such a good day that she wanted to share the experience about the brace installation with him. He picked up the call on the second attempt. "You're the one who held it steady."

They discussed everyday matters including weather conditions, the town service outage, and candle storage locations. He recommended she maintain a small notebook with essential numbers and contact information. "Solid," he said before she started speaking.

"It is," she said. "Thank you."

"The method helps you when your brain becomes exhausted," he explained. She recorded the information without any objection to following his instructions.

Later, she said she wanted to see him face to face.

There was a pause. "You do," he said with caution. "Just not the way you expect."

"That's not an answer."

"It's the only honest one I have."

She remained silent while the ocean continued to shape the coastline. The radio's exterior surface maintained a comfortable temperature which felt like the operation of an active device.

Next, she asked about his feelings regarding physical contact before she could stop herself. Anyone would have wanted to know what he looked like, and she knew it was a normal request.

"Yes," he said. "I miss the sensation of being present with someone when we didn't need any reason to be near each other."

Irene looked out the window that reflected her face in the fading daylight. The glass revealed her complete body shape, including her shoulder contours, mouth expression and hair pattern. She placed her hand on the table surface without touching the radio while her fingers remained close to it. The air in that spot had a slight warmth.

She spoke her words in a soft voice.

"You're living."

"That's new," she said.

"It shows."

The kettle made another sound when it finished cooling. She poured the remaining hot water from it into the sink before putting the pot back on the stove. The day had the right size. The space surrounding her felt like a perfect-fitting coat. Things were coming together.

She mentioned her plan to visit the library first thing in the morning to organize the mystery section and repair the loose card labels.

"Good plan," he said. "Take an apple."

"I will."

She turned off the lamp before leaving the window slightly ajar, as usual. The house kept its form in complete darkness without any external support. The space remained calm without any major events or sudden changes in temperature. Until she needed him to leave, the feeling of his presence persisted. He was with her.

She remained asleep until the next morning.

Chapter 7: The Storm

The next week came with unsettled weather — fog at dawn, sun by noon, wind by evening. It made the sea unpredictable, sometimes a mirror, sometimes a field of restless motion. Irene found herself matching its moods. One moment steady, the next uncertain. Changing your life is never easy, especially when you don't know exactly what kind of change you need or what one will fit for you. Things were so up in the air.

She worked her Thursday shift at the library. The small building smelled of paper, dust, and whatever polish Mrs. Dobbins used on the front counter. Irene spent the morning sorting returns and restacking the shelves, one of the most disliked activities no one else liked—nonfiction older than anyone asked for. Some books seemed to just sit in quiet solitude and wait for the lone reader who might come in and request it. Others were eagerly pulled from the shelves and rapidly re-stacked. Through it all, the quiet suited her. She could hear rain starting on the roof before she saw it through the windows.

Daniel stopped in just before lunch, carrying his usual tool bag and smelling faintly of cedar. "Door hinge," he said. "Catches on the bottom." Libraries needed fixing too, and he was here to do it.

She held the door open while he tightened the screws. His sleeve brushed her arm. It wasn't intentional, but she felt the warmth of it longer than she expected. When he straightened, their eyes met—brief, direct, then gone.

"That should last the season," he said.

"Thank you," she said.

"Harvest supper's on Saturday," he added. "You should come. They'll want music, and you've got a look that says you know at least one song."

"I don't," she said, smiling, "but I'll pretend."

"That's half the charm," he said, and left with a nod.

When he was gone, she stayed still for a while. The quiet didn't feel like rest anymore. It hummed with awareness. That small touch had somehow lit a spark.

That evening, the radio clicked softly before she'd even turned the lamp on.

"You're quiet tonight," the Voice said.

"I've been busy."

"I know," he said. "You're learning how people move around each other again."

"That's a strange way to put it."

"It's the right way," he whispered. "You've been living in the in-between. The world needs you back in its rhythm."

Irene ran a finger over the edge of the table. "I'm not sure it needs me. But it's nice to be seen again."

"You've always been seen," he said. "Just not where you were looking."

She hesitated. "Daniel asked me to the supper."

The pause that followed wasn't cold. It was deliberate—a breath held before an answer.

"You should go," he said finally.

"I thought you'd say that."

"You need the company of touch and sound. I can only give you one." But that bit of silence between his answer and her statement about going to this supper was a bit perplexing to Irene. Was the voice feeling something about that? She wasn't sure.

The honesty of it tightened her throat. "I don't want to hurt you." How can you hurt someone who's not even there? Someone who's a presence, but not a person. How do you do that? But she knew she cared for him and she didn't want to hurt his feelings.

He laughed softly, and the sound didn't carry sadness. "You can't hurt what's already gone, Irene. I told you, I stayed because I wasn't finished. Not because I wanted to be remembered this way." Finished with what? The question came to her mind, but she couldn't quite form it in order to ask. No, she didn't want to hurt him.

She looked at the small red light, steady on the dial. "What were you before this?"

"A man who forgot that love isn't meant to be held too tightly," he said. "The sea taught me that too late."

The air in the room changed, dense but gentle, like the weight before rain.

"You said once that you listen," she said. "Does it help?"

"It does when you speak."

They sat in the quiet. She could feel the air around her pulse with the faint hum that always followed his words.

"You sound tired," she said.

"Maybe I am," he said. "That's a good sign."

"How?"

"It means you're getting stronger. I won't need to hold on so close."

Her hand went still on the table. "Don't say that." Would he be leaving, and if he did, how would that be for her?

"It's not goodbye," he said. "It's growth. The hardest kind—the kind that means letting light in where there was only shadow."

The words stayed with her. She left the lamp on that night, the low bulb throwing a warm oval on the wall. When she closed her eyes, she could see both faces—the man in town who smiled without demand and the one she'd never seen who always knew what to say.

The morning when she awakened before dawn, it was raining. The cottage was dim in that light, the air cool against her face. She thought of the supper, of the small, unsteady hope that waited there. She made tea and didn't touch the radio.

At midmorning, the rain cleared. Daniel strolled up the gravel path with a roll of canvas and his affable grin. "You've got a leak starting above the porch," he said. "Thought I'd check it before it turns into a problem." Always helpful, never asking. Once he sees something, he attends to it.

She stepped aside, letting him in. "I didn't call."

"I know," he said. "But you were going to." Now he was beginning to act and sound like the Voice.

They worked together again in companionable silence. He balanced on the small ladder, careful but confident. She held the nails. The smell of damp wood and soap drifted between them. When the patch was done, he came down, brushing dust from his hands.

"That should hold through the winter," he said.

"I'm starting to think you fix things just to have an excuse to come by," she said.

"You're not wrong," he answered simply.

She laughed. "You're direct."

"I don't like guessing games," he said. "Life's short. I figure honesty saves time."

The words landed heavier than they should have. She nodded and looked away. "I'll see you Saturday, then."

"Good," he said, and left before she could say anything more.

When the door closed, she turned toward the radio. It sat quiet, the red dial dark. She stood there, waiting for a sound, a hum, anything. Nothing came.

"Are you still here?" she asked softly.

Silence.

She turned away, moved to the sink, and began washing the cups. The water ran hot; the steam clouded the window.

When she set the last cup down, she heard it—faint, steady, unmistakable. The hum returned, low and patient, like breath drawn near.

"I'm here," he said.

She let out the air she'd been holding in almost in anticipation and hope. "You scared me."

"I didn't want to interrupt," he said.

"You never interrupt."

"Maybe I should." Was he playing?

She sat down, leaning her arms on the table. "Don't make this harder than it already is."

"I'm not," he said. "I just want to remind you that the world outside your door is waiting."

"Why does it feel like you're pushing me away?"

"Because I have to," he said gently. "You've learned how to live with ghosts long enough. It's time to live with people again."

Her eyes stung. "Then what happens to you?"

"Nothing tragic," he said. "I'll still be here. Just less often. The sea has a way of reclaiming what it lent."

She pressed her palms to her eyes. "I don't want to lose this."

"You won't lose it," he said. "It will just stop needing words."

When she lowered her hands, the radio was dark again. No hum, no warmth. Only the faint sound of waves against the rocks.

She sat for a long time without moving. The clock ticked. The tea cooled. Outside, gulls cut sharp lines across the sky.

Then she stood, took her coat, and stepped outside. The path was damp but firm under her feet. The sea waited below, wide and shifting. She could hear its pulse, steady and familiar.

"Not lost," she said aloud. "Just changing."

The wind caught her voice and carried it toward the water. Somewhere in the distance, a low sound answered—not words, just presence.

And for the first time since she'd come to the cottage, Irene smiled without having to remember how.

Chapter 8: The Cost of Survival

The days shortened. By late October, the air turned sharp enough that the sea mist left a fine salt film on the windows. Irene learned to keep a cloth by the sill and wipe them each morning before the sun came up, but she did like the diamond shapes and glitter that it provided, even if it obscured the view. She'd stopped checking the weather report; she knew what kind of day it would be by the smell of the air before she even opened the door. Surely she had become a local, and she was as aware as they were of how the air foretold the weather for any day. That felt good. In fact, it felt good just being there. Finally, she was learning to feel what it was like to belong, to be liked, to be neighbors. And what was it all due to? Of course, the Voice played a role.

The routine gave her something to hold onto: mornings at the library, afternoons mending or writing in her aunt's ledger, and evenings by the fire. Some nights, Daniel stopped by to leave a jar of preserves or to ask how the roof patch had held through the last rain. The conversations were unhurried and easy. He never pushed, never asked about the things she didn't offer. Stopping by just seemed a natural thing for him to do, and she felt the same.

"You seem lighter," he said once, noticing the way she hummed while she wiped down the counter.

"I think I am," she said. "It's not gone, but it doesn't drag anymore."

He nodded. "That's how it happens. It doesn't leave. It just changes shape." Listen to how he was talking. It was almost as though he and the Voice were one now. They did share much in common with the way they spoke and how they encouraged her with what they said.

She thought of the Voice but didn't say his name. The radio hadn't spoken for three nights. Three nights seemed like an awfully long time for him to be silent. The red dial stayed dark, yet she still caught herself glancing toward it when the house fell too quiet. The absence wasn't frightening. It was... full, like silence in a church after the hymn ends.

That evening, she sat by the window, her tea cooling on the table beside her. Ocean waves and the tide were coming in fast, the waves heavier than usual, their white edges glowing faintly in the half-light. She could feel the shift in the air before the radio clicked on. As it did, she felt a small shudder go through her body, not in fear but in anticipation.

"Good evening," he said, voice low but clear.

Irene smiled before she spoke. "I was beginning to think you'd gone." Actually, she wanted to ask a lot of questions, but, again, she didn't want to interrupt whatever he was going to say.

"I've been near," he said. "Listening." Wasn't he always listening?

"I should've known," she said. "You never miss much."

"I've been watching the weather," he said. "The storms will come earlier this year."

"Then I'll seal the windows," she said. "And stay warm."

"Good," he said. "You're looking after things." He knew what was going on because he was always there, whether the radio glowed or not, and now she knew.

"I'm learning," she said.

A pause, not uncomfortable. The static softened like breath drawn in.

"I saw Daniel again," she said after a moment. "He's kind."

"I know," he said. "He fixes what he can, and he leaves what doesn't need it."

"You approve?" she asked.

"I do," he said. "He's careful with silence."

She looked down at her hands. "You sound... quieter."

"I'm tired," he said gently. "But it's a good kind of tired." What could he be tired from? She wanted to ask, and so she did.

"Because of me?"

"Because of what you've built," he said. "You've filled the space I was keeping open." Keeping open?

She felt a sharp ache in her chest, not fear, but recognition. "You make it sound like you're leaving."

"Not leaving," he said. "Just loosening. The tide can't stay at its high mark forever. It has to go out so the next wave can come in."

"I don't want you to fade," she said, her voice feeling small. Her voice felt like it had a note of pleading, and she didn't want to have him hear her like that, but it certainly felt like it to her.

"You don't need me as you did before," he said. "That's what love does—it teaches you how to stand in the quiet without needing rescue."

She looked toward the horizon, a thin band of silver between sea and sky. "And you? Who rescues you?"

"I think this was it," he said. "Finding someone who heard me and didn't turn away." So he did have feelings, and in a way, she had rescued him.

She closed her eyes. "That doesn't seem fair."

"It's enough," he said softly. "You gave back what time took."

They sat in silence, the hum of the radio barely audible, like a pulse fading into stillness. Irene pressed her fingertips to the edge of the table. It was warm—alive, but steady. Things were starting to fall into place.

"You were right," she said after a while. "About the pie. About the house needing to feel used. I never said thank you properly."

"You just did," he said.

She laughed softly. "That's cheating."

"I take what I can get."

The humor helped. It cut through the ache. She leaned back, letting her shoulders touch the chair. "Do you ever wish it had been different?" she asked.

"Every soul does," he said. "But the wishing isn't the work. The work is what we do after." It's amazing how he knew so much and how he could put it so clearly.

Irene looked at the window, where her reflection floated faintly over the dark glass. "What do I do after this?"

"You keep what matters," he said. "And you give away the rest." Sorting things out seemed to be his go-to suggestion.

The room grew very still. She reached out to adjust the dial, but her fingers hesitated. "If I turn it off, will you still be here?"

"I will," he said. "But not where you expect."

The words carried no drama, only peace. She lowered her hand and left the radio as it was. "Then I'll let you rest," she said quietly.

"Thank you," he said. "And Irene—when the first frost comes, plant something anyway."

"What would grow in that?" she asked.

"Hope," he said. "It's stubborn that way." Hadn't hope already been planted? After all, she now knew a man who had many of the qualities she needed and admired.

The red light dimmed until only its reflection remained in the windowpane. The room felt changed—not emptier, just wider, as if the air itself had stretched to make room for what she'd learned to feel.

Outside, a gust of wind brushed against the glass. The sea roared, distant but clear. She could tell by the rhythm that the tide had turned. Turned and carried him away? No, because he said he would always be there. And she supposed that meant watching.

When she went to bed, she left the radio untouched. She dreamed—not of voices or storms, but of a garden by the sea, soil dark and ready, frost melting from its edges. Someone stood there, indistinct, smiling. Did he also get into her dreams?

The next morning dawned still and pale. The cottage was quiet except for the clock and the slow settling of the boards. Irene opened the window. The cold air moved in, filling her lungs. It smelled like salt and something faintly sweet—like earth waiting for spring.

She smiled, pulled her sweater close, and whispered, "Good morning." No response, but she knew he was there somewhere.

The air didn't answer, but the warmth that rose behind her ribs said enough.

Chapter 9: First Sight

The season had turned again as it always would with such precision and prediction. The first cool edges of autumn crept into the calm evenings, and the sea took on its darker voice—lower, slower, and more deliberate. Irene had learned to sleep with the window open just enough to let that sound in. It had become her lullaby, her tether to everything that had brought her back from silence. Somehow, the sea was a friend that provided a soothing lullaby with its waves lapping the rocks and filling the evening with pleasant sounds.

Daniel was at the cottage often now. He was a quiet presence, content to read beside her or repair whatever the cottage's years had loosened. Sometimes, he would pause mid-task to look at her, and she could see the question in his eyes—not about the future, but about whether she was ready for it. When had she ever thought about the future when she was so busy trying to live in the present?

She was. Mostly. Yes, mostly ready for the future, but who's ever sure? The future is what the future is, she thought.

Still, some nights she woke suddenly, not from dreams but from a pull—a soft awareness that the veil between worlds had thinned again.

On one of those nights, the cottage was silver with moonlight, and she knew before she looked that the radio was glowing. He was back, or at least he was making his presence known if he wasn't ready to talk to her.

The red dial pulsed faintly, steady as a heartbeat.

She rose quietly, carefully and crossed to the table. The air felt charged—not cold, but full, as if every molecule was holding its breath.

"Is it really you?" she whispered.

"Yes," came the Voice—softer than she remembered, but unmistakable. He'd changed a bit, but just a slight bit.

She pressed her hand over her mouth. "I thought you'd gone." All this while, as she was proceeding through her life, she couldn't stop thinking of him and wanting to hear his voice again.

"I did," he said. "But not far. I promised I would return." Keeping his promise was something she was glad he did.

Tears glistened in her eyes. "Why now?" What could have happened that he suddenly decided he would return and in returning, he would have changed?

"Because you're ready," he said. "Because love that lingers too long becomes ache, and you have turned ache into motion." Did he know she was in love?

She sat down, trembling with a strange mixture of sorrow and peace. "I've missed you."

"I've been with you," he said simply. "Every time you laughed. Every time you reached out to someone new. I am in those moments, not in the walls or wires."

Her tears fell freely now. "It's different without your voice." What she was telling him was true, and she was revealing how attached she had become to him and his ability to help her continue on when things weren't clear.

"Then hear me another way." Another puzzle for her to solve, it seemed.

The air around her shifted, warm and dense. She felt it before she saw it—a nearness, as if the room had drawn close to her heartbeat. Then, beside the window, he appeared—faint at first, like mist shaped by memory. The outline of a man, tall and still, as though light woven into the air.

She didn't move.

"You're... beautiful," she said, the words breaking on a sob. Even though this was an apparition, and most times it would frighten her, now it was so pleasant, and she had so wanted to see him.

He smiled—she could feel it more than see it. "You always saw clearly, Irene. That's why I found you."

She rose, stepping closer, though she knew her body could never bridge that last inch. "Will I ever see you again?"

"In what matters," he said. "Through kindness. Through the sea. Through what you build next." He'd always be there in everything she did or said or even thought.

She nodded, unable to speak. The tears came harder now—not from grief, but gratitude. How could she tell him how wonderful it had been and how he had helped her to see the unseen and feel again? Whether she acknowledged it or not, she knew that he knew how she felt about her life before she came to the cottage and how it has changed now. He also knew that her feelings of grief for her sister were softening, but the memory would always be there, sweet and loving as it had been originally before she became ill,

He lifted his hand, and for an impossible moment, she felt warmth brush her cheek—like the gentlest wind, like light itself learning the shape of her face. Her heart skipped a beat, and in her mind, there was a wish, but she knew it could never be.

"Goodbye," she whispered.

He shook his head. "Not goodbye. Just peace."

The air brightened around him, gold and silver interlaced, and then—like a tide retreating into the horizon—he began to fade. She reached toward the vanishing shape, her hand finding only still air. Yet the warmth remained, lingering over her heart.

"Thank you," she whispered.

The radio gave one final click—soft, deliberate—and went dark.

Irene stood for a long time, the silence around her tender, not hollow. She turned toward the bed, climbed in slowly, wondering if this had all been a dream. But she knew it hadn't been a dream. And he was as real as real could be to her.

Irene lay awake a little longer, watching the silver wash of moonlight across the ceiling. There was no fear now, no loneliness. Only stillness—that rare, exquisite quiet that follows forgiveness.

Outside, the tide moved toward shore, the waves whispering in their endless rhythm: return, return, return.

Irene closed her eyes and whispered back, "I know."

And somewhere beyond the sound of water, a presence—unseen but felt—smiled and was gone.

Chapter 10: Love Never Lets Go

The morning again brought a soft gray light that followed the rainstorm to create a clean sky and salty air. Irene watched the ocean waves crash against the rocks beneath her window. The sea stretched out before her, but there was no sense of danger.

Daniel arrived to emerge from behind her and he met her gaze with a smile. "You're up early."

She had remained awake through much of the night because the moonlight was so bright in her bedroom. "I couldn't sleep," she said. "The light woke me."

He joined her by the window. "You're looking at the good light."

"The light brings me more than its brightness," she explained. Again she repeated, "It brings me more than its brightness." No, she wasn't going to explain to him about the Voice because that would remain between her and the Voice.

The two spent their morning in peaceful silence which they felt as a form of communication. Daniel repaired the shutter hinge that she had been putting off while she prepared scones that filled the cottage with sweet butter and baking aromas. During their meal, he took her hand across the table. She didn't pull away.

"What are you thinking?" he asked.

She told him in a soft voice that this moment felt perfect because the house seemed to have released all its tension. "As if the house has finally exhaled." How could she explain that to anyone? She hoped he would understand.

He smiled. "Then we'll let it breathe."

They walked along the beachfront barefoot while the cool wet sand touched their feet and squeezed between their toes. The sky was filled with gulls again and, as usual, they were making lots of noise as if to call each other or warn them to stay away. In the small tidepools around the ocean, there were hidden treasures, polished driftwood, glass-like stones and flat rocks. Irene picked up a small piece of sea glass that had a pale smokey color. She examined it under the sunlight as she rotated it. There was something beautiful about it, and yet she couldn't figure out why or where it might have come from.

Daniel watched her as she stood there. "You would want to keep that object." How did he know she was thinking about keeping this?

She nodded. "It's not perfect. But it's finished." Somehow, "finished" seemed to be the right word for this small piece of glass that must have been part of something bigger at one time. And now, being small was enough.

They stopped at the point where the waves touched the shore while she gazed toward the distant horizon. She spoke in a low voice about how she used to believe the ocean brought only destruction by taking things from people. "Now I think the ocean returns everything it takes but in different forms." The bit of glass was that something that was being returned in an altered, yet beautiful, new form.

Daniel turned and looked off in the distance, as she was doing right now. He followed her direction of sight. "Time operates in the same way as you described."

She smiled because she understood the truth behind his words. "We all exist as transformed objects that the ocean has reshaped."

His eyes sparkled with appreciation as he looked at her. "Your words sound like they belong in a book."

Again, she smiled while predicting that the words would become part of a book in the future. "Someday." Writing had always been something that attracted her, and now she believed she had something to write about.

While the sun started to set, they continued their walk until their shadows stretched across the beach. Off in the distance, the cottage interior awaited them like a beacon. Returning, they found it had transformed into a warmer space that seemed to hold sunlight after their return. The radio on the table was aglow in the last rays of the remaining light. But it was silent, and there was no reddish glow from the dial.

She ran her hand across its top as she would have a faithful pet or even a friend who had just awakened. "Thank you," she whispered. All she didn't say was in those two words, spoke volumes. No one had to tell her that the Voice was there, even if the radio showed no sign of him.

The following silence contained a gentle vibration from the radio, which seemed to have stored memories within wooden and wire parts.

But there were other things in their community to be considered now, and the two of them were going to have some fun together with the townspeople. The village residents gathered at the green space for their annual bonfire celebration that marked the end of the season. Children ran after sparks that resembled fireflies while Mrs. Dobbins played her fiddle with a joyful, happy look on her face. Daniel worked on the fire structure to make sure it would reach its highest point without any danger, while Irene assisted by adding wood to it as it rose toward the evening sky. It was a fire to light up the evening sky and send a glow all around those who watched.

The stars appeared closer than ever to her eyes as she looked up at the sky. This was an exceptional night, and she was feeling more special herself—not lost, but not regained, yet special.

She remembered her sister, her aunt, and the Voice that had crossed from beyond to lead her back home. She'd heard his final words through her inner understanding rather than through any physical medium. He had led her back as surely as if she had a guiding light leading the way.

"Live, Irene. Live well." Although she missed him, she would cherish his words and try to live well.

A single tear ran down her cheek while she hid her thoughts with a happy expression, keeping the precious feeling she had now when thinking of him.

Daniel reached out to touch her shoulder. "Are you feeling okay?" Of course he noticed the way she was looking off. And somehow he knew her pensive mood was different.

"Yes," she said while she took deep breaths to calm down. "I'm doing better than fine." The two of them stood watching the fire's embers jump into the night air and disappear while they gazed at the endless expanse of sky above them. Far off in the distant sky, one bright star seemed to twinkle more than the others.

Irene kept the window open that night, as usual, to let the air enter the house after she returned to the cottage. It was as though she was making sure a friend could enter this space and be welcomed all night long. Again, the ocean rocked with a steady and reassuring beat she recognized as her familiar heartbeat. The sea glass she'd found earlier was on the table reflecting moonlight, creating a soft trembling effect on the wall that matched her heartbeats. Even the glass seemed to welcome the moonlight.

The waves continued their eternal journey toward the shore while making a soothing sound that was beyond language.

Every voice she had ever loved seemed to exist within the sound that drifted from the ocean. Sleep came as a welcomed visitor as the night took over the cottage as though to protect it once again.

About the Author

P. A. Farrell is an accomplished flash fiction author whose compelling micro-narratives have captivated readers across the literary landscape. With over forty publications in prestigious online journals and literary magazines, Farrell has established herself as a master of the abbreviated form, crafting complete worlds and complex emotions within the constraints of brief word counts.

Her expertise in flash fiction extends beyond individual pieces to comprehensive collections, where she shows remarkable range and consistency in delivering powerful, bite-sized stories that linger long after the last sentence. Each collection showcases her ability to explore diverse themes, characters, and settings while maintaining the precision and impact that define exceptional flash fiction.

Farrell's work resonates with readers who appreciate literature that delivers maximum emotional and intellectual impact in minimal space. Her stories often examine the pivotal moments that define the human experience, capturing the essence of larger truths through carefully chosen details and expertly crafted prose. The breadth of her publication history speaks both to her prolific output and the consistent quality that editors and readers expect from her work.

Through her continued contributions to the flash fiction genre, P.A. Farrell has become a trusted voice for readers seeking literature that respects their time while enriching their understanding of the human condition. Her collections offer the perfect opportunity to experience the full range of her storytelling abilities in a single, cohesive volume.

In her other life, P. A. Farrell is a clinical psychologist who has written several self-help books and continues to contribute to media outlets such as Medium.com and Butterfly, where she posts articles on all aspects of healthcare, mental health, and a variety of other topics. Her Author's Page is here: https://tinyurl.com/4ewdunb8

Books by P. A. Farrell

Snowbound Hearts
   The Secrets We Keep
   The Secrets We Keep 2
   Whispers Across the Sea
   Love by the Latte
   Echoes of Expectation—Waiting
   Unexpected Short Tales of Surprise

A Special Request

I f this book has touched your heart, sparked your curiosity, or simply entertained you along the way, I'd be incredibly grateful if you could take a moment to share your thoughts with a review on Amazon or wherever you discovered this book. Your words not only help other readers find books they'll love, but they also mean the world to authors like me who pour their hearts into every page. Thank you for being part of this journey, and for helping stories find their way to the readers who need them most. Her Author Page on Amazon: https://tinyurl.com/4ewdunb8